The Adventures of Georgie and Bartholomew

Georgie Makes a New Friend

The Adventures of Georgie and Bartholomew

Georgie Makes a New Friend

Grandpa Lamaritz

LANIER
PRESS

LANIER PRESS

Alpharetta, GA

ISBN: 978-1-61005-794-3
Library of Congress Control Number: 2016957592

10 9 8 7 6 5 4 3 2   1 0 2 4 1 6

Printed in the United States of America

♾ This paper meets the requirements of ANSI/NISO Z39.48-1992 (Permanence of Paper)

Cover art and illustrations by Angela Brown

Dedication

To Aidan—
Thanks for helping me with the
original idea!

Long, long ago, when magic was normal and normal was magic, there lived a gingerbread man named Georgie. He lived in a house made of sugar cookies instead of gingerbread. Georgie often went walking in the woods alone to smell flowers, watch birds play in the trees, and listen intently to the babbling brook as it ran through the forest.

Most gingerbread men, as I'm sure you know, love to run through crowded towns playing tag or hide-and-go-seek. Not Georgie. He liked quiet much more than shouting and walking much better than running. Georgie didn't like doing anything that was expected.

One day, Georgie took a new trail—one he had not noticed before. Around a magical bend in the trail, he came to a wall made entirely of gumdrops.

The wall was very tall, and Georgie could not see over it. He walked along the wall until he found the gate. It was not locked. Georgie knocked first and then called out, "Helllooooo!" because it is only polite to knock and shout "Helllooooo!" before opening a gate that doesn't belong to you. No one answered, so Georgie opened the gate and peeked inside.

Off in the distance, Georgie saw a large nutcracker dressed like a soldier. Oddly enough, though, this fierce-looking nutcracker was picking daisies and

3

blueberries. Georgie called out again, "Helllooooo!"

The nutcracker looked up, waved, and said, "Helllooooo!" back to Georgie.

"My name is Georgie," Georgie shouted.

The nutcracker replied, "Mine is Bartholomew! It's nice to meet you."

Georgie was surprised by the fact that this nutcracker was so friendly. Most nutcrackers were such stiff people—never smiling, never laughing, and certainly

5

never picking daisies and blueberries. Georgie skipped over to where Bartholomew was working.

"How far does the gumdrop wall go?" Georgie asked.

"Forever," said Bartholomew.

"Surely not—because I've never seen it before, and I have walked through these woods hundreds of times."

Bartholomew replied, "Just because you haven't seen it doesn't make it not so."

6

Georgie had to think about that for a moment. He didn't know anything he hadn't seen. Surely Bartholomew was wrong.

As Georgie and Bartholomew were talking about things seen and unseen, they heard the sound of a large wagon coming by.

"Hide!" shouted Bartholomew. "It's the Toymaker!"

Georgie and Bartholomew ran and hid behind a thick clump of blueberry bushes.

"Why are we hiding?" Georgie asked.

"Because the Toymaker thinks I'm broken and wants to 'fix' me!" Bartholomew replied.

"What is broken?" asked Georgie.

"Nothing! He just thinks that a nutcracker is supposed to be serious all the time, never smile, and not pick daisies and blueberries," said Bartholomew, "but I love baking and eating blueberry muffins, and my kitchen is perfectly beautiful with vases full of fresh daisies all over the place."

"That doesn't sound like 'broken' to me," Georgie said. "It just sounds like 'different.'"

"Exactly!" exclaimed Bartholomew.

"People on my side of the gumdrop wall think I should live in a gingerbread house and run through the streets daring them to 'catch me if you can,'" said Georgie, "but I live in a house made of sugar cookies, and instead of running through the town, I walk through the woods and sniff flowers and listen to the brook as it tumbles over the rocks."

10

Unfortunately, while they were talking, neither one noticed the toy-repair wagon stop. The Toymaker got out, snuck up, and threw a large net over them. Soon he had scooped them up and was carrying them back to the wagon.

"Hey! Stop!" Georgie and Bartholomew cried, but the Toymaker ignored them and dumped them, net and all, in the back of the wagon.

"Quick, use your nutcracker teeth and chomp through the net!" Georgie cried to Bartholomew.

"I can't—my teeth are only painted on, and ropes don't crush like walnuts," Bartholomew replied.

And so, Georgie and Bartholomew bounced down the road in the back of the wagon, trying to figure out how to escape.

Finally, the Toymaker came into the center of a town Georgie had never seen. There were nutcrackers of all descriptions marching around or standing very still, all looking very serious, and all of them regarding Georgie and Bartholomew with very disapproving looks.

The Toymaker took Georgie and Bartholomew out of the wagon, into his toy-repair shop, and dumped them out of his net onto the rough floor.

"I don't know what to do with you," the Toymaker said to Georgie, "but I have a cousin who is a baker in the next town—I'm sure he can fix you up."

"But I don't need fixing! I'm not broken . . . I'm just different!" Georgie said.

"If you're not broken, then why aren't you trying to run away and shouting for me to catch you?" reasoned the Toymaker.

"Because I like to walk instead of run, and I sniff flowers and watch birds instead of playing tag," Georgie explained.

"Nevertheless, you sit quietly in the corner while I fix Bartholomew here," the Toymaker concluded.

"But I'm not broken either!" Bartholomew protested.

"Sure you are!" said the Toymaker. "You should be serious and standing at attention, not picking blueberries and making muffins!"

"Why?" asked Georgie.

"Because that's what nutcrackers do!" exclaimed the Toymaker, and he set to work on Bartholomew.

"Why?" asked Bartholomew.

"Because!" said the Toymaker with an exasperated tone in his voice.

"What if that doesn't make me happy?" asked Bartholomew.

"But it should make you happy!" said the Toymaker. "Everyone knows that toymakers are happy when they're making toys. Gingerbread men are happy when they're running away, and nutcrackers are happy when they're standing at attention and being serious. If that doesn't make you happy, there's something wrong and I need to fix it!" concluded the Toymaker.

"All I know," said Georgie, "is that no matter how you or your cousin, the baker, try to change Bartholomew and me, it won't work."

This was news to the Toymaker. He sat down to think about it. And he thought . . . and thought . . . and thought. The Toymaker thought about it for so long and sat so still that he fell asleep. Georgie managed to wriggle out of the net and crept over to the table where Bartholomew lay.

Georgie whispered, "Bartholomew! Are you okay?"

"Not exactly," Bartholomew whispered back. "The Toymaker has already removed my legs, so I'm stuck on this table until he puts me back together. You should run away before he sends you to the baker!"

"But that won't help you," Georgie pointed out. "You're still here, and he can still try to 'fix' you. We have to come up with a better plan."

"Aren't most gingerbread men really quick runners?" Bartholomew asked.

"Yes, but I really, really, really hate to run," Georgie replied. "I walk everywhere."

"And I hate to ask you, but just this once, would you mind running?" Bartholomew asked. "Run to my brother's house on the far side of the village. Maybe he can persuade the Toymaker to let me go," Bartholomew reasoned.

And so, for the first time in his long gingerbread life, Georgie ran. At first he was awkward at it, but he got better with every stride and was soon running faster than he believed possible.

Georgie ran through the town square and straight to the far side of the nutcracker town.

"Help me! Bartholomew's in trouble!" Georgie shouted at every nutcracker in sight. On his third try, Georgie found a

large, fierce-looking nutcracker who said, "I'm Bartholomew's older brother, Anthony. What kind of trouble is Barty in?"

Georgie explained as best as he could, panting heavily.

Anthony said, "Well, that will never do. He may not be the way I would like, but he's my brother, and no toymaker is going to change him to an unhappy nutcracker!

"Carl! Damon! Erica!" Anthony shouted, "Get the horses—Barty's in trouble!"

Georgie, Anthony, and his brothers and sister hopped on magical rocking horses and galloped to the Toymaker's shop.

When they arrived, Georgie and Anthony and his brothers and sister climbed down from their rocking horses and walked up to the Toymaker's door.

When they knocked on the door, the Toymaker opened it and looked out in astonishment at the crowd gathered at his door.

"What's the meaning of this?" the Toymaker demanded.

"We're here to rescue Bartholomew!" said Georgie.

"I don't need rescuing after all!" called Bartholomew from inside the Toymaker's shop. "The Toymaker and I had a long talk, and he agreed to fix me the way I wanted to be fixed rather than the way he had in mind."

"I've modified his hands to make it easier to pick blueberries and hold a basket," said the Toymaker, "and built a tall wagon with a daisy vase and space for lots of blueberries!"

And with that, Bartholomew showed off the changes the Toymaker had made and invited everyone back to his cottage for tea and blueberry muffins.

"I guess it's important to talk about what's wrong before you try to fix it," said the Toymaker after his fourth blueberry muffin.

"And it's important to know to ask for help when you need it," added Bartholomew.

"And the most important thing of all is to be happy being yourself," concluded Georgie.

It was all in all quite an adventure and quite a gathering of new friends.

Acknowledgments

Thank you to Julianna, my granddaughter, who has been telling me for twenty years to write down my stories.

Thanks also to Heidi, who patiently waited for Aidan and me to rough out the idea.

Many thanks to Linda, my wife, for believing in me and in the power of this story. I will do all I can to live up to your faith.

I continue to be amazed by and thankful for the patience and guidance of the Lanier Press staff through this whole process.

Above all, thanks to our creator for continually steering me back onto the path when I wander off!

35

About the Author

Grandpa Lamaritz was born in San Antonio, Texas. He and his wife, Linda, live in Bethlehem, Georgia. Grandpa currently has one granddaughter and two stepdaughters, who he hopes will provide more grandchildren in the years to come! Grandpa tries to live in accordance with his Christian beliefs and by the motto, "Find joy—spread joy—every day!"